RABBIT AND HIS FRIENDS

STORY AND PICTURES BY RICHARD SCARRY

A GOLDEN BOOK • NEW YORK

Western Publishing Company, Inc., Racine, Wisconsin 53404

One sunny morning, Rabbit found a roly-poly
egg outside his hole. "My goodness gracious," said
Rabbit, "Mrs. Hen must have lost one of her
eggs."

Something inside the egg was going *tap-tap-tap*.

"The egg is hatching!" said Rabbit.

And lickety-splickety, Rabbit ran off to tell Mrs. Hen.

"Mrs. Hen, Mrs. Hen, I found one of your eggs," shouted Rabbit. "And it's hatching!"

Mrs. Hen jumped up, all excited. "Cak, cak, cak, show me where," she cackled.

When they arrived, the egg had hatched. There stood the strangest animal that ever was!

"He doesn't look like any animal I have ever seen before," said Rabbit. "He has a big beak and little webbed feet just like Duck."

"He has a tail and a fur coat just like Beaver," said Mrs. Hen. "And he is very shy, like Squirrel.

"What are you, my dear?" asked Mrs. Hen.

But the roly-poly animal said, "I don't know."

Then splash, kersplash! that roly-poly animal jumped into the river and swam right down to the bottom.

"Did you see that?" asked Mrs. Hen. "Why, he swims just like Beaver, too."

"Who does?" asked a voice from behind them.

They looked up, and there was Beaver. So they both told him at once about the funny little roly-poly animal swimming under the water.

And just then the little roly-poly animal jumped out of the water and onto the river bank.

"My oh my," said Beaver. "He certainly has a tail and fur coat like mine. Tell me," he asked the funny little animal, "are you related to the beavers?"

"I don't know," said the little animal.

Pretty soon Duck and Squirrel came hurrying down the path.

"My oh my," said Duck. "He certainly does have a beak and webbed feet just like mine. Tell me," Duck asked the roly-poly animal, "are you related to the ducks?"

"I don't know," said the little animal shyly.

"My oh my," said Squirrel to himself, "it is plain to see he is shy as a squirrel."

Finally it got dark and they all had to hurry
home to supper. Away they all went, and the poor
little animal just sat there and wished he had a

nice warm home where he could have supper, too.
So he set off down the road to look for one.

Bright and early the next morning, Mrs. Hen
and Rabbit and Beaver and Duck and Squirrel all
hurried back to the river bank, hoping to see the
roly-poly little animal again.

But he was not there. Beaver swam down to the

bottom of the river, but the funny little animal
was not there either.

So away down the road they went.

Soon they came to a circus.

"What fun," they all said. "Let's stop to see the circus."

But when they reached the doorway, they found they could not go in. A big man was there, and he was shouting in a big loud voice, "Admission five cents. Admission five cents."

All Rabbit had was two cents and three buttons. All Mrs. Hen had was three safety pins. Squirrel had a jackknife and four cents. And Beaver had only his handkerchief. Duck didn't have anything at all. So they could not go in to see the circus.

They were all so sad because they couldn't go
to the circus.

"What shall we do?" said Mrs. Hen.

And just then, what do you think?

They heard a funny little voice say, "Let them
in, please. Let them in to see the circus. They are
my friends."

Quick as a wink, the big man let them all in.

And who do you suppose had spoken to him?

It was the roly-poly little animal. He was
sitting up on a big platform.

He was all dressed up in a beautiful striped bathing suit. And in one of his webbed forefeet he had an ice cream cone. In the other he had a great big lollipop.

On the platform with him he had a diving board and a swimming pool where he could go swimming whenever he liked.

"How did you get up there?" asked Rabbit.

"When the circus man met me on the road last night," said the roly-poly animal, "he was so happy to find me. He told me that I was a real live platypus. And that I was the rarest and most interesting animal in the whole world. And then he told me that I could be in his circus and have my own swimming pool."

"Look," said Duck proudly. "He has a duck bill and four duck feet like mine."

"Yes, and he has a tail and a fur coat just like mine," said Beaver.

"And he came out of an egg just like one of mine," said Mrs. Hen.

Squirrel was too shy to say anything, but he was happy because the roly-poly platypus was just as shy as any little squirrel.

And Rabbit was happy and proud that he had found Platypus down at the bottom of that deep, dark, muddy hole.

And the roly-poly platypus was very, very happy because he was like all the other animals, and they were all his friends.

SEE
THE PLATYPUS

THE MOST WONDERFUL ANIMAL IN THE WORLD

A FRIEND OF RABBITS, HENS,
SQUIRRELS, DUCKS, BEAVERS,
AND OTHER ANIMALS
AND ESPECIALLY
OF LITTLE GIRLS AND BOYS

Admission Is Free to
All Friends of the
Roly-Poly Platypus

COME ONE! COME ALL!